Sally Gardner is the author of the Fairy Catalogue, The Glass Heart, A Book of Princesses and other popular books for children, as well as the Magical Children series. She started out as a designer of sets and costumes for the theatre. She has a teenage son and twin daughters and lives in London.

ALSO BY SALLY GARDNER

The Invisible Boy
The Boy Who Could Fly
The Boy with the Magic Numbers
The Smallest Girl Ever
The Boy with the Lightning Feet

Lucy Willow

The Glass Heart
The Fairy Catalogue
Fairy Shopping
The Real Fairy Storybook (text by Georgie Adams)
A Book of Princesses
Playtime Rhymes
The Little Nut Tree

I, Coriander
The Red Necklace
The Silver Blade

THE STRONGEST GIRL IN THE WORLD

Sally Gardner

Orion
Children's Books

*To Diani Belli for
all her love and friendship*

First published in Great Britain in 1999
by Dolphin paperbacks
Reissued 2002 by Dolphin Paperbacks
an imprint of Orion Children's Books
a division of the Orion Publishing Group Ltd
Orion House
5 Upper St Martin's Lane
London WC2H 9EA

An Hachette UK company

The author would like to thank Jane Fior for all her help.

A catalogue record for this book is available
from the British Library

Printed in Great Britain by Clays Ltd, St Ives plc

The Orion Publishing Group's policy is to use papers that
are natural, renewable and recyclable products and
made from wood grown in sustainable forests. The logging
and manufacturing processes are expected to conform to
the environmental regulations of the country of origin.

www.orionbooks.co.uk

1

Josie could do many tricks. She could balance a pencil on the end of her finger. She could pick her nose without anyone seeing. She could tickle the cat until it said Stop it! But her best trick happened at ten-thirty one Friday morning. It was a trick that changed her life.

It happened in the school playground when Billy Brand got his head stuck in the school railings. His teacher, Mrs Jones, came to help. It was no good. Billy Brand's head would not budge. The school nurse came to have a look. Billy Brand was going very red. The headmaster, Mr Murray, called the fire brigade. The dinner lady put butter on Billy Brand's swollen face but still he could not squeeze his head through the railings. Billy Brand was well and truly stuck.

All the children crowded round to have a look. This was the best fun they had had all week.

"Will he explode, miss?" asked a little lad.

"Miss, miss, will they have to cut off his head?" asked another.

"No," said Mrs Jones. "Now, children, please don't all crowd round."

Billy Brand started to cry.

It was then that Josie Jenkins, aged eight and nine months, knew that she could do her trick. She felt a whizz of power down her arm into her fingers.

She went over to the iron railings and bent them right back. It was like pulling tissue paper apart, easy-peasy. Billy Brand's head was no longer stuck. There was a stunned silence, then a loud cheer. Mrs Jones couldn't believe her eyes. There stood Billy Brand, a little red in the face, with butter on his ears, but free.

At that moment Mr Murray came running into the playground, followed by the fire brigade. All the children were now trying to see if they could bend the school railings, which they couldn't. Billy Brand was standing in the middle of them looking rather red and silly.

"What is the meaning of this?" said Mr Murray, looking at Billy Brand. "How did you get free? Mrs Jones, what is going on here?"

Mrs Jones, who was quite lost for words, pointed at Josie. "Well," said Mr Murray, "is this some kind of trick?"

"Yes, sir," said Josie. "I could see Billy was stuck so I just unstuck him."

The fire officer was looking at the bent school railing. "Who did this?" he asked.

"I did, sir," said Josie.

Mr Murray looked as if he might explode at any minute.

"Josie," he said, "those railings are made out of iron. No one can bend iron, especially not an eight-year-old girl. That is why I called the fire brigade."

"Shall I straighten them out again, sir?" asked Josie.

"Don't talk such drivel!" said Mr Murray.

Josie walked over to the railings and in front of the whole school, in front of the fire officer, she gently put the railings back as they were.

2

That evening Josie was having tea with her
family, Mum, Dad and big brother Louis. She
hadn't told anyone about what had
happened at school. She had a small feeling
that no one would believe her. Even Mrs
Jones, her teacher, had told the whole class
that it was just a trick that Billy Brand and
Josie had thought up between them. Billy
Brand had had to stand all afternoon
outside Mr Murray's door. Josie had had to

write a hundred times I won't do any more tricks.

"You're very quiet, my love," said Dad. "Everything all right?"

"Yes," Josie mumbled. She thought there was a chance her dad might understand about the school railing. He often told her that magic is all around us except people don't want to see it. But as for Louis who was twelve and clever, best to keep quiet.

After tea and telly, Josie went to her bedroom. She just had to see if she could still do her trick. She picked up her bedroom chair. It was as light as a pencil. She was just balancing it at the end of her finger when Louis walked into her bedroom. Usually Josie hated Louis barging into her bedroom. But not tonight.

"Josie, what are you doing?" he laughed. "Trying to be the strongest girl in the world? Come on, put the chair down before you hurt yourself." Josie put the chair down gracefully and with no trouble at all.

"You do it, Louis," she said.

"Oh, give us a break. Pick up a chair! That is so easy, it's sad! But if it makes you happy…"

Louis picked up the chair. It was much heavier than he thought. There was no way he could balance it on one finger. Then he nearly dropped it. Finally he banged it down heavily on the floor. He was not going to let his baby sister show him up. He went over to Josie and patted her on the head. "That's a good girl. Time for bed."

For once Josie was not cross with Louis. She knew her trick hadn't gone away.

The next morning Josie was up and downstairs before Louis. Her dad was eating his breakfast. "Well Josie, my love, off to watch the cartoons?"

"No Dad," said Josie. "I want to help you at work today."

Josie loved where her dad worked. He owned a small garage where he mended old cars. She would always take him his lunch on a Saturday and he would push his tools off the bench so that his little princess could sit next to him and not get dirty. But she had never before gone to work with him. That was Louis' job.

"All right," said Dad, "you can answer the phone and make us coffee." It was not quite what Josie had in mind but it would have to do. She waited all morning until her chance came.

"I'm just popping out for a minute with

Louis. Answer the phone if it rings and don't touch anything."

Josie went over to the car her dad had been working on. This was what she had been waiting for. Would her trick work on cars as it had on the school railings and on her chair? She put her tiny arm out and held on to the bumper of the car. Then she lifted. Yes! Yes! she could do it. The car was no heavier than her school rucksack. With a bit of careful handling she could balance it on the palm of her hand.

That was how Dad and Louis found her: this skinny little girl in a dress holding up a Ford Cortina.

"Don't move!" screamed Dad. "Louis, call 999 and get the fire brigade fast."

Josie carefully put the car down. "Don't call them," she said. "They don't like my tricks."

4

The rest of the day Dad and Louis tested Josie's so-called trick. There was no doubt about it. This little girl was amazingly strong.

"You're all very quiet tonight," said Mum as they ate their tea. "Cat got your tongues?"

Dad cleared his throat. "Joan," he said, "there is something we have got to tell you."

"Oh Josie," said Mum. "You didn't fiddle with anything in the garage?"

"No," said Dad, "nothing like that. It's just – well – Josie is probably the strongest little girl in the world."

Her mum burst out laughing until tears rolled down her face.

"Oh, Ron, you say some daft things."

Dad gave Josie a wink and she lifted the tea table up as though it were a book and swirled it around on her finger. Mum sat back in her chair, as white as a newly washed sheet.

"That's nothing," said Louis with pride. "My

little sister can lift a car that would need a crane and..."

"Hold on a minute," said Mum. "Are you telling me that our little girl, who is small for her age, and skinny to boot, who looks as if a gust of wind could blow her away, can lift a car?"

"Yes," said Josie. Then she told her mum about the school railings.

"Well, what do we do?" said Mum. "I mean,

who would believe it?"

"We do and say *nothing*," said Dad. "We keep it to ourselves for the time being."

"You don't think she should see a doctor?" said Mum.

"Oh, Mum," said Louis. "Josie's fine. She's just amazingly strong."

"Well, Josie," said Mum, "you're still my little girl, strong or not." And she gave her a big hug.

Josie was not looking forward to Monday morning. In class assembly, Mr Murray, the head teacher, gave a talk on the wrongs of showing off, and playing silly tricks in the playground. Even her teacher, Mrs Jones, still seemed to be cross with her. Worst of all, she was now the butt of all the jokes.

"How does it feel to be a hairy strong girl?"

"Hey, here comes Superman's sidekick."

It went on like this all day. Only Billy Brand stood up for her.

"That's it," thought Josie. "Dad's right." Best to keep this trick to herself.

Never had Josie been more pleased to hear the home bell ring. There was her mum waiting for her.

"Ready for tea, love?" said Mum.

"Not half," said Josie. "It's been a really bad day." They walked out of the school playground towards the main road. That's when it happened. That's when nothing would quite be the same again.

A van came charging out of control down the hill towards the zebra crossing, towards Josie and her mum and all her chums. The driver was running behind it, shouting as loud as he could. Nothing was going to stop it. Josie had that whizzing feeling in her arms and without another thought she ran into the road, putting her skinny arm at the

18

ready to stop the van. It was no heavier than catching a football and a lot easier on account of its size. The van stopped in its tracks, no damage done. There was a moment of stunned silence while the crowd took in what had happened. Then chaos. Mums and dads fainted. The lollipop lady went dizzy and the owner of the van couldn't believe what he had seen.

When the police and the ambulance arrived,

they thought there must have been an awful accident; there were bodies lying all over the place. The lollipop lady was mumbling something about a little girl. The van driver was sitting on the pavement saying it must be magic. The poor policeman in charge didn't know what to think. And there standing in the middle of the road was a little girl holding on to a van.

"Are you all right?" said the policeman.

"Oh, fine," said Josie, "but I can't let go because it could start to roll again."

They're all mad, thought the policeman. He said, "It would be a good idea if you got out of the road and left that van alone."

Josie did as she was told.

"Now," said the policeman, taking a notepad from his jacket. "Can anyone tell me what happened?"

But before the policeman could write a line, the van started to roll away again.

Josie ran back into the road and stopped it for the second time.

"Thank you," said the policeman. "Now, where was I?"

It took quite a lot of clear thinking on Mum's part to stop the policeman from taking Josie down to the police station for further questioning.

6

At home Dad was pacing up and down the living room carpet.

"I am sorry," said Josie. "I just did it without thinking."

Her dad looked up. "Poppet, you did the right thing. You are a very brave and strong little girl."

"Nothing will happen, will it?" said Josie, looking at her dad's worried face.

"No, it's just that the paper will get hold of the story and I don't know what they will make of it."

The doorbell rang. "Hello, Mrs Jenkins," came a soft-spoken voice. "My name is Avril Ghoast and I'm from the local paper, the *Echo*. I wonder if I could have a word with you about your daughter?"

Josie stood in the living room with Mum and Dad, looking small and worried in a pretty dress and shiny shoes. Avril Ghoast was sure that this was all a huge joke. No one would believe that this will-of-the-wisp could stop a bike, let alone a van.

"It's a joke, isn't it?" said Avril, looking at Mum and Dad. "Sorry to waste your time. This is my first job as a reporter and I suppose the lads at work thought it would be a bit of a laugh to send me here."

"Well then, the laugh's on them," said Dad.

"Ron, no," said Mum, "I don't think we should say anything."

"It's no good, Joan," said Dad. "It's out now.

The best we can do is let Avril know the true story, not some made-up nonsense."

That is how Avril Ghoast made her first huge break as a journalist. A photographer from the *Echo* came to photograph Josie lifting the Ford Cortina. It was headlined in the local paper. It was headlined in the national papers too.

The next day a TV crew turned up to film Josie. The TV reporter wore trendy glasses.

"We need to see this on film," he kept saying. "I mean, how do we know that this is not a trick?"

"It *is* a trick," said Josie. "It's my best ever trick."

The TV reporter gave a nervous laugh. He turned to Dad and said, "I have just got back from India where I was supposed to film an elephant lifting a car. When I got there, the elephant wouldn't or couldn't do it. I was left with the whole village saying they saw the elephant lift the car on Tuesday or was it a truck on Wednesday. I came home with nothing. I bet," he added, looking glumly at Josie, "this is just another White Elephant story."

"Can I change before I lift the car again?" said Josie.

"Do what you like," said the TV reporter, fiddling with his glasses. "I'm sure it won't make the slightest difference."

"Well then," said Dad, "I think you will be in for a bit of a shock."

Josie put on her prettiest party dress, brushed her hair and put on one of Mum's old hats. When the TV reporter saw her, he didn't know whether to laugh or cry.

"I'm a bit fed up with lifting the same old car.

If it's all the same to you, could I see if I can lift a bus?"

"A bus," repeated the reporter. "Why not! Let's do a bus."

They all trooped down to the local bus station. "Which do you fancy?" said the TV reporter, looking at his watch. "I haven't got all day."

Josie went over to an empty double decker bus. This would be the biggest test of her trick yet. She went round to the front and lifted it up on to her shoulder without any trouble. It weighed no more than an empty rucksack. Josie pushed the bus up until she was balancing it on the palms of her hands.

"This is wonderful! Oh my word!" shouted the TV reporter, who seemed suddenly to have come to life. "I am standing in the bus station with Josie Jenkins who is eight years old and probably the strongest little girl in Britain, in the world, in the universe..."

Josie liked this. She took one hand off the

bus and straightened her hat. She wanted to look her best. She had never been on television before. The main news story that night was about Josie Jenkins' incredible strength.

7

Stanley Arnold, the strongest man in Britain, was watching the news that night. He didn't find the story about Josie Jenkins very funny. Who was this little girl who had the cheek to go about lifting up cars and buses, that's what he wanted to know. He called his agent. "What is all this nonsense about Josie Jenkins?"

A few squeaks could be heard down the phone.

"I don't care what you say. I want to show everybody that this little upstart is having us all on." A few more squeaks came out of the end of the phone. "No one, I repeat no one, is stronger than Stanley Arnold. I want a competition. That will show her up for the fraud she is."

No one argued with Stanley Arnold. He ate beef wholesale.

"You don't have to do this silly competition, poppet," said Dad. But Josie was cross. "How dare he say that I'm having everyone on!" she said.

"I'll kill him," said Louis. "He has no right to be so rude about my little sister."

"Now," said Mum. "Shall we all just calm down. Josie doesn't have to go in for any competition. She doesn't have to prove anything to anybody."

"Especially not to Stanley Arnold," muttered Dad.

But Josie liked the idea of a competition. It gave her a good tingling feeling just to think about it.

Stanley Arnold went in for serious body building. Josie went shopping and bought some very pretty shoes that she had been wanting for ages.

The day arrived. It was held in a football stadium so that the crowds could get in. Stanley Arnold arrived with his agent, his personal trainer, his publicity lady and his fan club. Josie arrived with Mum, Dad and Louis.

"Well, on looks alone, we know who's won," laughed Dad. "Now Josie, don't go hurting yourself. Stop at any time."

The competition was divided into three parts. First part: dragging a car for three metres. Second part: throwing a barrel over a wall. Third part: a tug of war.

Stanley Arnold went first. He dragged his car, going red in the face, every muscle in his body ready to pop. But he got the car across the finishing line. The crowd roared. A commentator said it was Stanley Arnold's fastest time.

Now it was Josie's turn. She walked over to the car, sucking a lollipop. She had lifted them up lots of times but she had never walked with a car. The huge crowd went quiet. Josie lifted the front of the car and

balanced it on one hand, like a waiter
holding a tray. She walked past Stanley's car
to the other side of the football pitch, still
sucking her lollipop. The crowd went wild.
Stanley Arnold looked even wilder. The
commentator said Josie Jenkins had broken
all known records.

Next was throwing the barrel over the
wall. This is what Stanley Arnold did best. In
fact he was famous for throwing the barrel.

He took a long run, then, with a grunt, let
go. The barrel went high into the air and
landed with a loud bang behind the wall.
The crowd went crazy. The commentator
went crazy. "This is a world record for
barrel throwing."

Then it was Josie's go. She picked up the
barrel and threw it as if it was a tennis ball.
The barrel whizzed higher and higher up
into the air, so high that it could not be
seen. Then, like a rocket, it hit the ground,

making a huge crater. The crowd was silent. The commentator said in a quiet voice of disbelief, "Josie Jenkins has broken all known world records for barrel throwing."

The Grand Finale was the tug of war. Stanley Arnold had been sprayed down. He flexed his muscles and chalk was put into his hand. For extra grip, Josie pulled up her socks.

The rope was very thick. Josie took one end and before she was ready, Stanley gave a mighty pull. Josie landed in the dirt and grazed her knee. The crowd booed.

The referee walked on to the pitch. Josie pulled herself up. She thought Stanley Arnold was very rude.

"On the count of three, pull..." yelled the referee.

One, two, three. Josie grabbed hold of the rope. The whizz in her arms was so powerful that it was like

pulling the string on a kite. Stanley Arnold, the strongest man in Britain, felt his feet leave the ground as he spun round and round the football pitch. It was a sensational victory. There could be no doubt that this was the strongest girl in Britain.

Stanley Arnold got into his large car and went home, saying it was an insult to his strength to perform with a human freak.

Josie hadn't changed one little bit. But her life had. Before her trick there had been time to play with her friends, to watch videos with Louis. Now hardly a day went by without someone wanting Josie to show off her incredible strength.

It had been good fun at first. Her teacher, Mrs Jones, had said she was sorry for not believing Josie, and so had the headmaster. None of the children teased her. In fact, she was quite a star; a star to everyone in fact except the person she really wanted to impress - Louis. Why couldn't he see this was her greatest trick ever? Instead, he was constantly putting her down. "Not much skill in lifting cars," he would say, or "You'll end up with muscles like Popeye's."

Louis didn't like Josie's trick one little bit. He was fed up with everyone talking about his baby sister. In truth, Louis was jealous, green with the stuff. Heck, he used to be the strong one. He used to be responsible for his little sister. How could he look after the strongest girl in the world? Only Superman's older brother would know how Louis was feeling. That's if Superman *had* an older brother, which he didn't.

Then came an offer that would change all their lives. Mr Two Suit flew in from New York just to see the girl with the mighty strength.

The Jenkinses had

never met anyone quite like Mr Two Suit before. He had a face like a potato and a fake flower where his heart should have been.

"The offer," he said, smiling his most charming smile so that his two gold teeth shone, "is this. I take you and your family to New York to do some serious shopping!"

It sounded like a fairy tale. Mr Two Suit pulled a fat envelope from his front pocket. "Fame and fortune will be yours, Mr and Mrs Jenkins. Just sign the contract here, if you please."

Dad signed. How he could he refuse? They'd never been further than Blackpool.

9

New York was amazing, with buildings so tall they could talk to the stars.

41

"This is well wicked," said Louis. They were staying in the Plaza Hotel in their very own suite.

"There are more rooms here than we have at home," said Mum.

There were flowers everywhere. A bath the size of a swimming pool. Room service on tap.

"This is the life," said Dad.

Sam Two Suit had got Josie a publicity lady, a clothes designer, a hairdresser, a manicurist, a personal trainer and a chauffeur with a stretch limo to take them wherever they wanted to go.

Josie was transformed, with puffed-up hair and a frilly shiny dress. Mum and Dad looked barely recognizable. Louis looked just about all right.

"What have they done to you, Josie? You look like a living doll," said Louis.

Josie agreed but she wasn't going to let on to Louis. "I think I look pretty," she said.

"Yes, pretty awful," said Louis.

"That's enough of that," said Mr Two Suit, "I love it, the camera will love it, and the public will love it. Just think of the Look Alike Dolls we'll be able to sell."

But Josie didn't feel right. She didn't feel like Josie Jenkins.

The next morning Josie was photographed lifting up a car outside the Plaza. The picture appeared on the front page of several newspapers. The headline read: *Josie Jenkins age 8 challenges America to find someone stronger!*

10

As it happened there was no shortage of people willing to pit their strength and their money against Josie Jenkins.

The first of many challenges took place on a beach on Long Island. Josie was dressed in a designer swimsuit and was wearing a hat. She was to beat the record for carrying cement-filled barrels from a raft in the bay back to the shore. Mum didn't like the look of this at all.

"She could drown, Ron," she wailed, "lifting those barrels."

"Joan," said Dad, "for goodness sake! Josie is going to be fine. What is a cement-filled barrel compared to a car?"

There was one small problem. The raft had been put too far out in the sea. Josie couldn't stand up. However, this was put right and Josie managed to arrange her cement barrels in neat building blocks

which needed a crane to take them down.

"Things are going great," said Sam Two
Suit. "Tomorrow you've a date to pull a
truck, princess. That'll wow them!"

Josie wasn't listening. She was longing to

go swimming with Louis.

"Last one into the sea is a green banana!" she shouted, about to run into the waves.

"Hold it right there, princess," said Mr Two Suit. "The strongest little girl in the world doesn't play. She trains. That's why I have provided you with a gym and a personal trainer."

Of course, Josie had never used a gym or a personal trainer. It wasn't *that* sort of a trick.

11

It wasn't long before Mr Big Country
himself took up the challenge. He bet more
dollars than sense that Josie couldn't lift his
horse off the ground.

Quite a crowd turned up on the day, plus
a TV crew. This was a story worth filming.
Mr Big Country was big. His horse was big.
Josie was small, very small indeed.
Mr Two Suit rubbed his chubby
hands together.

"It'll make a great picture,"
he said.

"But next time, I want her in a designer dress."

"It's not the dress that matters," said Mum anxiously. "It's that horse."

"Quit the whining, Mrs Jenkins, and smile. You're on camera," said Mr Two Suit, grinning.

Mum couldn't smile. She was far too worried. "She could get badly hurt," she said.

Mr Two Suit wasn't interested. He was looking at the future. His future paved with gold, with Josie making him the richest man in the world.

The horse turned out to be a calm and well-behaved animal who longed for his owner, Mr Big Country, to sweep him off his hooves high into the air.

Mr Big Country puffed himself up like a turkey, then lifted his horse a few centimetres off the ground. The crowd clapped politely, the horse looked disappointed and Mr Big Country gave a satisfied smirk. He was famous for lifting up his horse.

"Beat that, little girl, if you can," he said.

Josie wasn't sure. Her dad tried to sound upbeat. "You can do it, poppet," he urged, though to tell the truth he could see how Josie might feel that her trick wasn't up to lifting a live animal.

Suddenly Mr Two Suit's vision of the future became horribly clear. He could see himself losing a lot of money. He wasn't about to allow this to happen. No two bit horse was going to stand in his way to fame and fortune.

"Lift that horse, Josie Jenkins," yelled Mr Two Suit. "I order you to lift that horse."

"This is crazy," said Mr Big Country. "That skinny kid couldn't lift a candy bar. I think you owe me one mighty big cheque!"

It was at this moment that the horse whispered something into Josie's ear. Then, to everyone's amazement, she lifted the horse by his hind legs as high as she could, which was a lot higher than Mr Big Country had managed.

The horse snorted. He had waited his whole life for this moment. He reared into the air with Josie holding on tightly and stayed there for what seemed like forever. The crowd went crazy. The film crew couldn't get enough of it. Finally, with a smile, Josie put the horse gently down.

Mr Big Country looked rather small as he handed over his money to Mr Two Suit. The horse on the other hand was one happy animal. This was something to boast about to his friends in the stable.

12

It soon became clear that Josie Jenkins and her family were nothing more than a circus act and Mr Two Suit the greedy ringmaster. Every day there was a new city, a new challenge. It all flashed by so fast that soon the challenges merged together in one large blur.

At first Dad had loved all the razzamatazz that surrounded Josie. He felt like a star trainer as he urged Josie on to yet more incredible feats of strength, but pretty soon he, like Mum, became worried that Josie really would hurt herself. Josie's parents began to think that it had all got out of hand

HOLLYWOOD

and should be stopped. Louis agreed. He longed to get back and see his friends and his home again. He didn't like having to live in the goldfish bowl of publicity. As for Josie, the star of it all, what she wanted was to do something useful rather than these endless challenges that helped no one. Superman saved people, didn't he? The world, the universe, that sort of thing. He hadn't ended up as part of a circus act. If this was all she could do, she would rather go home.

"How is it that such a great trick can go so wrong?" she asked Louis gloomily. They were in their hotel room listening to Mum and Dad arguing next door.

Mum was saying, "Enough is enough, Ron."
Then more muffled words from Dad.

"And what about the garage?" said Mum.
"You'll lose all your customers if they find
that their cars haven't been mended."

"I know," shouted Dad. "But what can we
do?"

What they did was tell Mr Two Suit they
were going home.

13

"Home!" said Mr Two Suit, rolling the sound in his mouth like a gobstopper. "Home," he repeated slowly as if waiting for it to change colour. He glowered at Josie. "You can't," he said flatly. "I own you, the lot of you. I own Josie Jenkins Incorporated. You," he said, pointing at Dad, "signed the contract. If you break it, Mr Jenkins, I'll sue you for every penny you have. Do you understand?"

They understood all right. They were well and truly caught in Mr Two Suit's net. In no time at all, he had Mum and Dad bundled off to Florida to a Home for Irritating and Worrisome Parents. They didn't even get the chance to say goodbye. Louis was allowed to stay with Josie as long as he was good.

So here they were, stuck on the twelfth floor of the Plaza Hotel, Louis and Josie by themselves and with no way of getting home.

Josie looked miserable and Louis gave her a hug.

"Don't worry," he said. " We're in this together, And somehow we are going to get out together."

14

Louis had a plan. It was quite simple. At the first opportunity that came along, Josie would talk to the TV reporters and tell them what had happened, and how they wanted their mum and dad back so that they could go home.

The next day Mr Two Suit came in. He was very excited.

"I have a major deal! A breakfast cereal company wants you to star in their commercial. All you have to do is lift this three storey house, lock, stock and barrel, and move it to a new site."

"Why?" said Louis. "That sounds daft."

"Look, wise guy, I am getting pretty sick of you," said Mr Two Suit. "If you can't put a sock in it, I'll send you away too."

"No!" shrieked Josie.

"Sorry," said Louis.

Mr Two Suit turned to Josie. "Filming being

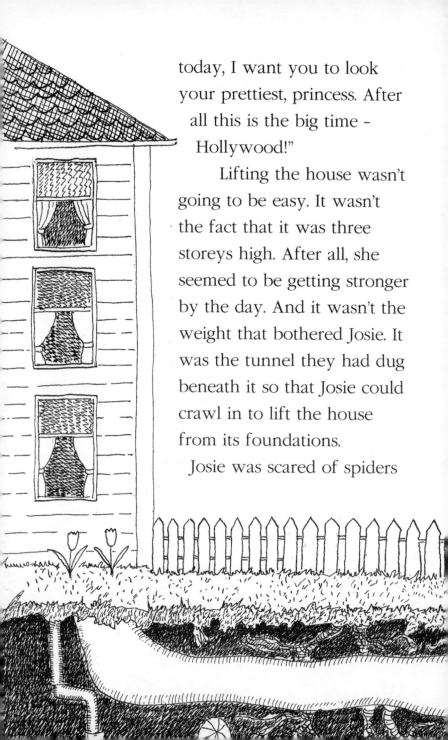

today, I want you to look your prettiest, princess. After all this is the big time – Hollywood!"

Lifting the house wasn't going to be easy. It wasn't the fact that it was three storeys high. After all, she seemed to be getting stronger by the day. And it wasn't the weight that bothered Josie. It was the tunnel they had dug beneath it so that Josie could crawl in to lift the house from its foundations.

Josie was scared of spiders

and she was worried about all the crawly insects that would appear, like when you lift up a stone. Mr Two Suit couldn't care less.

"For heaven's sake, what's your problem? How can a few insects frighten the strongest girl in the world? Give me a break!"

"We would like to get started," said the lady director, "so can we have some action."

"I will go in with Josie," said Louis.

"Oh *thanks*," said Josie, taking his hand and giving it a squeeze.

Louis crawled in first with a torch to make sure there were no spiders. Josie went in next. He

looked at his little sister. She seemed so small and the house so big. He was just about to say "What are we doing?" when he realized that daylight was shining in.

Josie had the house balanced perfectly on her shoulders. It wasn't heavy but it was a bit difficult to walk and hold the house at the same time. Louis guided her carefully.

"A bit more this way... yes, you're doing fine."

Josie managed to walk the house down the street to where the very fussy woman who owned it was waiting.

"No, don't put it here, honey. I want it a bit more to the left," she said.

"Look," said Louis. "This is a three storey house my sister is carrying, not a beach chair."

Josie put the house down without breaking a single window pane.

"Cut," said the director. "That was just wonderful. The bit with your brother helping was so touching."

"It's in the bag, Josie," said Mr Two Suit. "The ad company were thrilled. In two days' time, we go to Hollywood!"

Louis and Josie were not thrilled. There had been no reporters to talk to so their plan hadn't worked so far.

"There'll be another chance tomorrow," whispered Louis. "Don't let's give up hope."

15

Their chance came sooner than they could have possibly imagined. There was a major disaster. One of the main support cables of the Brooklyn Bridge had come loose. Cars and buses were stuck, no one daring to move in case the whole bridge came down. The television was running all day bulletins. New York was brought to a standstill. In the Plaza Hotel, Josie and Louis sat glued in front of the screen.

"All those poor people," said Josie. "What will happen to them?"

"Oh, turn it off," said Mr Two Suit, "and let's get down to business. We have without doubt the silliest and easiest challenge of them all. This dad has contacted me and bet half a million dollars that you can't lift his son's rucksack. What a punk! It will be like stealing candy from babies."

"Why does he want me to do that?" said

Josie. "It sounds silly."

"Because he thinks one day your strength will give out. What a fool."

"But what about those people on the bridge?" said Louis.

"What about them? It means nothing to me. There's no money in people stuck on bridges."

"I'm going to get some sweets from the lobby. Are you coming, Louis?" said Josie.

Before Mr Two Suit had time to stop them, the phone rang.

"This is the plan," said Josie as they were going down in the lift. "I know it sounds a bit silly but I think I could help with that bridge."

Louis had been thinking the same thing until he had seen the pictures on TV. The bridge was an awesome size.

"Oh Josie, that really would be some trick," he said. "But are you sure?"

"Not really," said Josie, "but it's worth a go."

"It sure is," said Louis, smiling.

The lobby was full of people, all milling around, waiting for news about the Brooklyn

Bridge. Josie and Louis made their way to the hall porter. They had decided that he was their best bet because he had a kind, understanding face. At first, he hadn't the faintest idea what these two kids were talking about until it finally sunk in that the little girl in front of him wanted to help. He nearly burst out laughing, then he looked at Josie again. After all, this was Josie Jenkins, the little girl with the amazing strength. Perhaps it wasn't such a silly idea after all.

"What about your boss?" he asked.

Louis begged him not to tell Mr Two Suit

because if he knew that Josie was offering to do this out of the kindness of her heart, he would go bananas.

The hall porter looked quickly round the lobby, then he ushered them into a little room and told them to stay there until he got back.

Louis and Josie waited for what seemed like ages.

"I bet he's phoned Mr Two Suit. We'll be in big trouble," said Louis.

Just then the door opened and the porter reappeared.

"Don't say a word," he hissed. "Just do what I say. Mr Two Suit is on the war path, looking for you."

The porter hurried them out of the front of the hotel. To their amazement a helicopter had landed in the hotel grounds. Josie and Louis were rushed on to it and the door slammed to. As they rose high up into the sky, they could see the chubby little figure of Mr Two Suit waving his arms.

It gave Josie courage to see
him looking no bigger than
an ant.

16

Garth Griffen was in charge of the rescue services. So far he had the fire brigade, the police, ambulances and a number of helicopters at his disposal but nothing could be done. The whole thing was balanced on a knife edge. If they airlifted people off the Brooklyn Bridge, panic could break out. And if the balance was altered the whole bridge might collapse. And then there was the tide to think of. Garth Griffen was at his wits' end. The last thing he needed was an eight-year-old girl and her brother on the scene.

"This is a national disaster, not an adventure playground," said Garth.

"I am Josie Jenkins," said Josie very firmly.

Oh, he knew who she was all right. This was the girl with the mighty strength and the silly dresses. But a car was one thing – this was a huge bridge. Garth Griffen wasn't about to take any chances.

"What I need is some delicate lifting gear which should be here before the tide changes, not an eight-year-old girl," he said.

At that moment a call came through. There was a problem with the crane. It wouldn't be there for three hours.

"Oh great! Just great!" said Garth. "We don't have three hours. What we do have is a little girl!"

He looked again at Josie. This was madness. Heck,

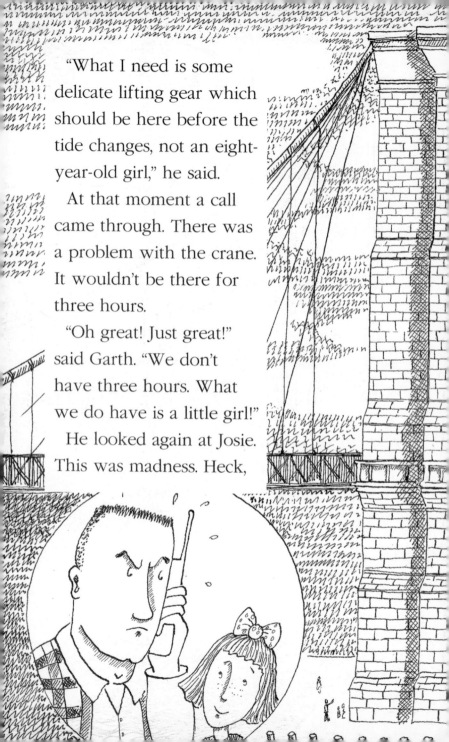

he was a father of four. He knew all about girls. They could do many wonderful things but lifting Brooklyn Bridge? He doubted it.

"Look," said Louis. "I am not saying that she can do it, but surely it is worth a try."

Garth scratched the top of his head. Oh, what had he to lose? Nothing else seemed to be working.

Josie was put into protective clothing which was too big for her. So was Louis. "I don't leave Josie's side," he said.

"We're a team," said Josie proudly.

They were taken up to the top tower of the Brooklyn Bridge. Josie could see quite clearly where one of the suspension cables had given. Far down below the bridge was rocking dangerously back and forth in the wind. The cables were groaning loudly as if about to snap. It was all very scary.

Josie suddenly felt very unsure. The bridge was so massive. Would her trick be up to this?

Louis gave her hand a little squeeze. "Good luck," he said.

At that moment a whizz went down her arms, even more powerful than the whizz she had had when Billy Brand got his head stuck in the railings.

Josie put her feet apart and got ready to pull. Garth Griffen looked at this little girl thinner than a runner bean, then back down to the bridge. This was madness. He was just about to say "Forget it, it's not going to work," when he realized that little by little Josie was pulling the slack cable until the bridge was straight.

"Let's get those people off," ordered Garth, "and quickly."

The bridge was heavy, but not so heavy that she couldn't keep her grip. Far down below Josie could see the rescue services getting people to safety.

Louis kept saying encouraging things. "This is a pretty awesome trick, you know," he said. He had never been so proud of her.

Josie kept the bridge straight for a grand total of forty minutes. When she let go. everyone clapped and cheered. Garth Griffen put her on his shoulders and TV reporters rushed up to get the full story.

"How do you feel?" they shouted, pushing their cameras and microphones up to her face.

"I am pleased," said Josie, "that my trick has done some good." Then she carried on bravely, "Ever since I came over here, I have done nothing but silly things."

"But surely," said a lady reporter, "you are pleased with the fame and fortune that your challenges have brought you."

That was when Louis spoke up and told the reporter how they were nothing more than prisoners of Mr Two Suit.

"You did it!" said Josie. "You told everyone. Now Mum and Dad will come back and we will be able to go home."

But unfortunately Louis' appeal for help was cut due to the commercial break.

17

When they got back to the Plaza, Mr Two Suit looked as if he might explode with rage.

"You go out of the hotel without my permission and fix some piddling bridge that I told you wasn't worth a dime, when we could have made half a million bucks."

They were grounded; locked in their room without supper, without television, nothing. They both felt very down when the phone rang. Josie answered it and to her

amazement
found that
she was
talking to
Stanley
Arnold.
He was in
Florida doing
a strong man

competition and he had turned on the news
and blow him down! there was little Josie
Jenkins. He was ringing to congratulate her
and to ask whether there was anything he
could do. She had only to ask.

Josie told him all about Mr Two Suit and
what had happened to Mum and Dad.

Stanley Arnold was a man of few words.

"I'll see you tomorrow, kids," he said.

18

The next morning Josie woke up and knew that something was different. She felt strange, heavy, as if her bones were made of lead. She got out of bed and then she knew. Her trick had gone, had disappeared as suddenly as it had come. She couldn't even lift the bedroom chair.

"I can't do it any more, Mr Two Suit," said

Josie. Mr Two Suit was not in a listening mood. He just wanted Josie looking pretty and down in the Palm Court in fifteen minutes.

"All you have to do is lift that little rucksack," he said.

Josie felt very small. She wanted Mum and Dad. She wanted to go home. When Louis came in, he found her in tears. The minute he looked at her, he knew that something had changed.

"Louis, my trick has gone," said Josie.

"It doesn't matter," said Louis. "At least you won't have to do any more stupid challenges."

Josie sobbed, "I tried to tell Mr Two Suit but he wouldn't listen. He said I had to be down in the Palm Court in fifteen minutes. What am I going to do?"

Louis wiped Josie's eyes. "Look, it was a great trick while it lasted," he said, "but you are much more than your tricks, Josie. Don't you see? Mr Two Suit can't do anything to us now. We'll be able to go home."

Josie brightened up. "You really think so?"

"Yes Josie, I do. I'm glad that your trick has gone away." And he took Josie's hand and together they went down to the Palm Court.

There they found a very tall, spotty lad, fifteen years old, with his very tall father. The rucksack was full of large, heavy encyclopedias. When Josie tried to lift it, she couldn't get it off the ground. There was a gasp of disbelief from the guests who had gathered round to watch. Mr Two Suit yelled, "Stop playing about and lift that rucksack!"

Just then Dad pushed his way to the front of the crowd. Josie couldn't believe her eyes. She ran towards him, tears rolling down her face.

"Dad, oh Dad, I can't do it any more."

"Never mind, princess," said Dad. "It doesn't matter. Come on, Louis, we're going home."

Dad lifted Josie up and took her to Mum who was standing at the back with Stanley Arnold. Louis and Josie had never been so pleased to see them.

"Oh thank you, thank you, thank you," Louis was saying to Mr Arnold.

"Very touching," said

Mr Two Suit. "Now if you would like to step this way, I think we have some serious talking to do."

Mum, Dad, Josie, Louis and Stanley Arnold followed Mr Two Suit into the lift up to their suite.

"I don't want him in the room," said Mr Two Suit, looking at Stanley Arnold.

"That's all right," said Stanley. "I'm waiting for a friend so I'll just stay in the corridor until he comes."

"We are going home," said Dad. "We have had enough of your monkey business. There was nothing in the contract about Josie losing her strength."

"Oh, very clever," said Mr Two Suit. "A short plane ride with Stanley Arnold and you are suddenly experts on contracts. You can leave and go home, by all means, when you have paid the bill."

"What bill?" said Mum. "Josie earned you lots of money. In fact, I think you might owe us something."

"Very funny," said Mr Two Suit, not laughing. "I have just written out a cheque for half a million dollars for a rucksack. And how much do you think staying in the Plaza costs? And your vacation in Florida, Josie's clothes, her hair, her food, her fitness trainer? Who do you think pays for that? YOU DO, you jerks."

He handed over a bill. "This is how much you owe me." Mum and Dad turned white. They had never seen so many noughts in their lives.

"There must be some mistake. I mean, we can't possibly owe this much," said Dad.

"Believe me, you do," said Mr Two Suit.

At that moment, Stanley Arnold entered the room. Behind him stood a very smart gentleman with tiny gold-rimmed glasses.

"May I introduce my lawyer?" said Stanley.

Mr Two Suit was about to say something but didn't. Stanley Arnold was, after all, very big and very strong. No one messed with Stanley.

"The contract if you please," he said. Mr Two Suit handed it over.

"I think," said the lawyer, looking hard at the piece

of paper, "that we will talk in the other room."

The Jenkinses and Stanley waited anxiously. They could hear raised voices, then all went quiet. They were in there for ages. Then the lawyer came back.

"There's bad news and there's good news," said the lawyer. "The good news is that you don't owe Mr Two Suit anything."

Dad and Mum gave a loud hip, hip, hurray.

"The bad news is that because it was a truly dreadful contract, he doesn't owe you anything either except your air fare home. I am sorry that I can't do more for you."

"Oh thank you," said Dad. "It doesn't matter about the money. We just want to be able to leave."

Stanley Arnold shook Josie's hand. "You are a very strong little girl with or without your trick, Josie Jenkins, and I wish you all the best. As for you, young man," he said, turning to Louis, "I take my hat off to you for looking after her so well."

"Hear, hear," said Mum and Dad.

Mr Two Suit booked them on to the very next plane to London. He couldn't wait to get rid of them. He had just heard news of a boy in Russia who could fly.

Josie sat in the lobby while Dad went to see if he could find a taxi. No more stretch limos.

"What are all these people doing?" said Mum. Louis looked at the crowd of people coming their way. He recognized the face of Garth Griffen. In the middle of the huge group was a very important-looking gentleman.

"May I introduce myself?" he said. "I am the Mayor of New York."

"Very pleased to meet you," said Josie politely, feeling a bit baffled. The mayor smiled. "On behalf of this great city, we would like to thank you for your bravery and for your selfless courage in saving so many from a possible disaster." A loud cheer went up. "To show our gratitude to you and your remarkable family, we would like you to accept this humble cheque as a sign of our appreciation."

Josie looked at the cheque in disbelief. There were even more noughts on it than on Mr Two Suit's bill. Josie jumped up with joy and gave the mayor a kiss. Cameras clicked.

"Thank you," she said. Everybody clapped.
It was quite a little party.

They were taken to the airport in the
mayor's own limousine and were flown first
class to London.

19

It didn't take long for everything to get back to normal. Josie was thrilled to see her house and her friends. She was even excited about going back to school. Billy Brand was pleased to see her and so was Mrs Jones. They all said that she had been missed. Dad and Mum were their old selves again and

Dad's customers forgave him for the late repairs on their cars.

Louis was just pleased that everything was how it used to be. It seemed to him that New York had been a dream except for one thing. He and Josie now got on really well and hardly ever fought. As for Josie, she didn't mind that she was no longer the strongest little girl in the world.

She didn't miss her trick one bit. She was glad to be plain Josie Jenkins, now eight but soon to be nine years old.